THIRD-GRADE DETECTIVES

The Clue of the Left-Handed Envelope

By GEORGE E. STANLEY

Illustrated by SALVATORE MURDOCCA

ALADDIN · New York London Toronto Sydney New Delhi

This book is dedicated to the wonderful

students in Mrs. Schlueter's third-grade class at

Lincoln Elementary School in Norman, Oklahoma.

You're great! Thanks for all your help.

First Aladdin Paperbacks edition October 2000

Text copyright © 2000 by George E. Stanley
Illustrations copyright © 2000 by Salvatore Murdocca

A Ready-for-Chapters Book

Aladdin Paperbacks
An imprint of Simon & Schuster Children's Publishing Division
1230 Avenue of the Americas
New York, NY 10020

26 28 30 29 27 25

ISBN-13: 978-0-689-82194-3 (pbk.)
ISBN-10: 0-689-82194-8 (pbk.)

Library of Congress Control Number: 98-10579
0816 OFF

Chapter One

It was the first day of the third grade, and Noelle Trocoderro was late.

She ran down the sidewalk outside the school building.

All summer long, Noelle had been looking forward to starting school again.

Mrs. Trumble would be her teacher this year.

Everyone loved Mrs. Trumble.

She was the nicest teacher in the whole school.

Finally, Noelle reached Mrs. Trumble's third-grade classroom.

She stopped at the door.

There was a *man* writing on the chalkboard.

Something's wrong here, Noelle thought.

She looked around.

Her friend Todd Sloan was waving to her.

Todd lived across the street from Noelle.

They did a lot of things together.

Noelle thought Todd was more interesting than most of the girls in her class.

She hurried over and sat down in the empty seat next to him.

"Who's that man?" Noelle whispered.

"Mr. Merlin," Todd replied. "He's our new teacher."

"What happened to Mrs. Trumble?" Noelle asked.

"She moved," Todd said. He leaned closer to Noelle. "Amber Lee Johnson said Mr. Merlin used to be a spy."

Noelle blinked. "How did she find that out?"

Todd shrugged.

Noelle looked at Mr. Merlin again.

She liked spy shows on television.

Maybe she wouldn't miss Mrs. Trumble after all.

Mr. Merlin stopped writing on the chalkboard.

He turned around and faced the class.

"Good morning, class. I'm Mr. Merlin. I'm your new teacher," he said. "I used to be a spy."

Leon Dennis raised his hand. "What did you do when you were a spy?"

"I caught lots and lots of other spies," Mr. Merlin said. "I used lots and lots of secret codes, too."

Todd leaned over to Noelle. "Amber Lee said he did those things in *foreign countries,*" he whispered.

Noelle looked at him. "Really?" she whispered back.

Todd nodded.

"Going to school is like solving a mystery," Mr. Merlin continued. "We're going to solve a lot of mysteries this year."

"What kinds of mysteries?" Amber Lee asked.

"All kinds," Mr. Merlin said.

He looked around the classroom.

"Does anyone here have a mystery we can start with?" he asked.

Noelle sighed.

She wished she had a mystery so she could impress Mr. Merlin.

"I have a mystery," Amber Lee said.

"What's your mystery?" Mr. Merlin asked.

Amber Lee stood up.

She waved an envelope at everyone.

"This came for me in the mail yesterday," she said. "I want to know who sent it."

"What does it say?" Mr. Merlin asked.

Amber Lee took a letter out of the envelope and started reading.

"'Dear Amber Lee, you are the smartest girl in the world.' It's signed: 'An Admirer.'"

She looked at Mr. Merlin.

"If I knew who sent it," she said, "I could say thank you."

Mr. Merlin smiled.

Noelle rolled her eyes at Todd.

"That's not a mystery," she whispered. "Amber Lee probably sent that letter to herself."

Todd nodded his agreement.

"Okay," Mr. Merlin said. "We'll solve the mystery of who wrote Amber Lee the letter."

He turned around.

He started writing on the chalkboard.

He wrote:

$$\begin{array}{ccc} E & E & N \\ P & X & V \\ O & L & E \end{array}$$

"But first you all have to solve a secret code," he said.

"Why do we have to do that?" Leon asked. "Why can't we just solve the mystery?"

"Secret codes are fun," Mr. Merlin said. "They also help you learn to think better."

"I already know how to think," Leon said. "I don't like to do it too much."

"Well, you'll want to think about this," Mr. Merlin said. "There's a clue in it that will tell you where to start so you can solve the mystery."

Chapter Two

"That looks easy," Amber Lee said.

Mr. Merlin smiled.

Amber Lee is such a show-off! Noelle thought.

She looked around the room.

Everyone was busy trying to solve the secret code.

Noelle raised her hand.

She had to wave it around several minutes before Mr. Merlin saw it.

"Yes?" Mr. Merlin said.

"I think it looks easy, too," Noelle said.

Mr. Merlin smiled again.

Amber Lee gave Noelle a dirty look.

"I don't think it looks easy," Todd whispered.

Noelle didn't think it looked easy, either, but

she wasn't going to admit that to anyone.

Mr. Merlin let them work on the secret code for fifteen minutes.

When the time was up, nobody had solved it.

Mr. Merlin stood up.

"If you're a spy, you may have to solve secret codes without any help," he said.

"But sometimes you have a codebook to use.

"The codebook has rules to follow.

"I'll give you three rules for this secret code."

Great! Noelle thought. If she had the rules, she was sure she could solve the secret code.

Then she could solve the mystery.

Mr. Merlin wrote the rules on the chalkboard.

He wrote them next to the secret code:

1. The middle of the clock is X.
2. You need to start at noon.
3. You should follow the hands.

Noelle studied the rules carefully.

The middle of the clock is X.

What clock was he talking about? she wondered.

She saw an *X*, but she didn't see a clock.

You need to start at noon.

Did that mean they had to wait until noon?

No! Mr. Merlin had told them to work on it now.

You should follow the hands.

What hands? Noelle wondered. She didn't see any hands, either.

She sighed.

She rested her chin in her hands.

From where she was sitting, she could see the big clock on the wall of the classroom.

She always liked to watch the big red second hand as it raced around the numbers.

It made her think that. . . .

She stopped.

That's it! she thought.

She raised her hand.

"I can solve it, Mr. Merlin!" she said excitedly.

Chapter Three

Amber Lee stood up. "She can't solve my mystery!" she cried.

"Amber Lee!" Mr. Merlin said. "Please sit down!"

He took a deep breath.

"Remember that you're the one who asked the class to solve your mystery," he said.

Amber Lee sat down.

She rolled her eyes at the ceiling.

"Oh, okay," she said.

Mr. Merlin looked at Noelle. "You may tell us what you think the secret code says."

Noelle walked to the front of the room.

She smiled at everyone.

She even smiled at Amber Lee.

She tried to make it a nice smile.

Amber Lee pretended to read a book.

"This secret code was very hard," Noelle said.

"I thought and thought and thought and thought and thought and thought and thought and thought and thought and—"

"Okay, Noelle. We get the picture," Mr. Merlin said. "Please continue."

"Finally, when I saw the big red second hand on the clock," Noelle continued, "I knew how to do it.

"You pretend that X is the middle of a real clock.

"If you start at noon, that means you start at twelve o'clock.

"On a real clock, twelve would be the middle E on the top line.

"If you follow the hands, then you write the letters the way the hands on a clock would go: $E N V E L O P E$

"The secret code clue is *envelope!*"

"Excellent!" Mr. Merlin said.

He held up the envelope that Amber Lee's letter had come in.

"To solve this mystery, you need to start with

the envelope," Mr. Merlin said.

"What's so special about the envelope?" Amber Lee asked. "It just looks like a plain old envelope to me."

Mr. Merlin turned around.

He started writing on the chalkboard again. He wrote:

A S B
L X A
I V A

"Here's a new secret code clue," he said. "It'll tell you something you need to know about the envelope."

"*Sbaavila!*" Amber Lee cried.

The class laughed.

Mr. Merlin smiled.

"Good try, Amber Lee," he said. "But this is a different secret code."

Noelle had started to say *sbaavila,* too.

She was glad she hadn't.

But now she didn't know what this new secret code clue meant, either.

13

"Here are some new rules," Mr. Merlin said.

"The middle of the clock is *X*.

"You need to start at noon.

"You should go the other way."

Noelle raised her hand.

"Salivaab!" Amber Lee shouted.

"Excellent!" Mr. Merlin said.

Noelle knew it, too.

She wished she had just shouted it out like Amber Lee had.

"But leave off the *ab* at the end, Amber Lee. Those are just the first two letters of the alphabet," Mr. Merlin said. "They're only used to fill up the square."

"Saliva?" Misty Goforth said. "What's that?"

"Spit!" Todd said. "It's spit!"

"Oh, yuck!" Amber Lee said.

Noelle frowned. *What did spit have to do with solving this mystery?* she wondered.

Chapter Four

Noelle had just started to ask Mr. Merlin that question when a woman knocked on the door of the classroom.

Mr. Merlin looked up.

"Come in, Dr. Smiley!" he said.

Dr. Smiley came into the classroom.

"Class, Dr. Smiley is a scientist. She works for the police," Mr. Merlin said. "I asked her to tell you all about what she does."

Dr. Smiley smiled at the class.

Then she told them how she used science to solve crimes.

When she finished, she said, "I'll even show you how I do it one of these days."

The class applauded

Todd looked over at Noelle.

"I didn't know policemen were so pretty," he whispered.

"She's not a police*man*," Noelle said. "She's a police*woman*."

"Actually, she's a police *scientist*," Todd said.

Noelle thought Dr. Smiley was pretty, too.

"I wonder if Dr. Smiley and Mr. Merlin are a couple?" she whispered. "She keeps smiling at him. Only couples smile at each other that way."

"I'll ask," Todd whispered.

He raised his hand.

"No, Todd! You don't ask people things like that!" Noelle whispered. "I'll find out some other way."

She looked over at Amber Lee.

Noelle was sure Amber Lee would know.

Amber Lee seemed to know everything about everybody.

Noelle would have to ask her.

Amber Lee liked it when people asked her questions.

✉   ✉   ✉

The rest of the day, they did their schoolwork.

When the final bell rang, Noelle and Todd left the classroom together.

"I asked Amber Lee if Mr. Merlin and Dr. Smiley were a couple," Noelle said.

"What'd she say?" Todd asked.

"She didn't say anything," Noelle said. "She just grinned."

"She knows," Todd said. "I know she knows."

"You have to come to my house," Noelle said. "We have to solve this mystery before Amber Lee does."

"Why are you so worried about this mystery?" Todd asked. "I'm getting bored with it."

Noelle looked at him. "You've always liked mysteries before. Why don't you like this one?"

"I don't care who sent Amber Lee that stupid letter," Todd said.

"But I need your help, Todd. If Amber Lee solves the mystery first, people really will think she's the smartest girl in the world. She'll never let me forget it, either."

"Oh, all right," Todd said.

When they got to Noelle's house, Todd called his mother to tell her where he was.

Then he and Noelle went to Noelle's room.

"Okay," Todd said. "What do we do first?"

"We think about envelopes and spit," Noelle said. "Those are the two clues that Mr. Merlin gave us."

So they thought about envelopes and spit for several minutes.

Then suddenly Noelle jumped up.

"Of course!" she shouted. "Come on!"

She started out of her room.

Todd was right behind her.

They went downstairs to the den.

Noelle opened the bottom drawer of a big desk.

She took out a big box of envelopes.

"Now we can solve this mystery," she said.

"How?" Todd asked.

"You use spit to lick envelopes," Noelle said. "So we'll lick all of these envelopes until we figure out what the mystery is."

"That is so dumb, Noelle," Todd said.

"No, it's not. My dad does it all the time," Noelle said. "It's called *trial and error.*"

"What does that mean?" Todd asked.

"It means you have to keep making mistakes over and over until you get it right," Noelle said.

They went back upstairs to Noelle's room.

Noelle handed Todd an envelope.

"You start," she said.

Todd stuck out his tongue.

He licked the flap.

"Ugh!" he said. "That glue tastes awful!"

He looked at Noelle.

"Did you notice anything when I licked it?" he asked.

Noelle sighed. "Nothing. That must have been an error." She picked up an envelope. "Watch me."

"Okay," Todd said.

Noelle licked the flap of her envelope.

Todd was right, she thought.

The glue tasted awful.

"What happened when I licked the flap?" Noelle asked.

"Nothing," Todd said. "I guess it's another error."

"You didn't see anything that would help

us solve the mystery?" Noelle said.

Todd shook his head. "No."

"We're missing something here," Noelle said.

"We have spit.

"We have envelopes.

"Those are the two things Mr. Merlin said we needed to solve the mystery."

She sighed.

"I guess we'll just have to keep licking these envelope flaps and watching each other until we figure something out."

They took turns watching each other lick envelope flaps.

Finally, there were no more envelope flaps to lick.

"I don't have any more spit in my mouth, anyway," Todd said.

"Me, either," Noelle said.

She looked down at the floor.

It was covered with envelopes.

They were all stuck together.

Noelle just hoped her parents weren't planning to write any letters soon.

"Now what?" Todd said.

"Maybe Mr. Merlin will give us some more clues tomorrow," Noelle said. "I just hope that Amber Lee hasn't already solved the mystery."

Chapter Five

Noelle hurried down the sidewalk toward Mr. Merlin's classroom.

When she reached the door, she stopped.

"Please don't let Amber Lee have solved the mystery," she whispered.

She held her breath.

Then she slowly went inside.

She looked over at Amber Lee.

She let out her breath.

She knew she could relax now.

Amber Lee didn't look very happy.

In fact, Amber Lee looked really mad.

Noelle was sure that meant Amber Lee still didn't know who had sent her the letter.

Suddenly, someone touched Noelle's shoulder.

She whirled around.

It was Leon.

He was holding a glass jar.

"Spit in this jar," Leon said.

"*What?*" Noelle cried.

"Spit in this jar," Leon repeated.

"Why?" Noelle demanded.

"I need some of your spit," Leon said.

"No!" Noelle said.

She went on into the classroom.

Leon followed her.

"Spit in this jar, Noelle!" Leon whispered. "I have to have some of your spit!"

Noelle took her seat next to Todd.

She ignored Leon.

Finally, he walked away and took his seat.

"What's going on?" Noelle whispered to Todd. "Why did Leon want me to spit in that jar?"

"Amber Lee is having some of her friends collect spit for her," Todd whispered. "She said that's what police do. She saw it on television last night."

Noelle wondered if she should be collecting spit, too.

She decided she just couldn't go around

asking people to spit into a glass jar.

She looked around.

Several people in the class were holding glass jars.

Noelle could see the jars had something in the bottom of them.

Spit!

For a moment, she thought she was going to be sick.

Then the bell rang.

And Mr. Merlin started class.

"Did anybody solve the mystery?" he asked.

"I've almost solved it," Amber Lee said. "My friends and I are collecting spit from everyone."

Mr. Merlin blinked. "Would you care to explain that, Amber Lee?" he said.

Amber Lee stood up.

"It's what police do," she said. "I saw it on television last night."

"Well, it is true that police detectives often collect saliva samples from suspects," Mr. Merlin said, "but you have to be very careful about doing that because of diseases."

"Ugh!" Amber Lee's friends cried.

They all dropped their glass jars.

The glass jars fell to the floor.

Now, there was spit and glass all over the place.

Several people screamed.

They put their feet up on their desks.

Noelle saw Mr. Merlin take a deep breath and let it out.

But he didn't get angry.

Instead, he sent Leon to get the janitor.

While the janitor was mopping up the floor, everyone copied the day's spelling words off the chalkboard.

When the janitor finished, Mr. Merlin said, "Now, then. Back to our mystery. What are the rest of you doing?"

Noelle raised her hand.

"Yes?" Mr. Merlin said.

"Todd and I licked all of the envelopes at our house last night," she said. "We watched each other. But we didn't notice anything unusual."

"Well, you and Todd are on the right track, Noelle," Mr. Merlin said.

Noelle smiled.

Amber Lee frowned.

"I'll give you another clue," Mr. Merlin said. "To solve this mystery, you really do need to start with saliva, but it's the saliva on the flap of Amber Lee's envelope."

Amber Lee gasped.

"Let's do an experiment," Mr. Merlin said. "I have envelopes for everyone."

He passed out the envelopes.

"Hold them up in front of you," Mr. Merlin continued.

All the kids in the class held up the envelopes in front of them.

"On three, I want everyone to lick the flaps," Mr. Merlin said. "Ready? One, two, *three!*"

Noelle licked the flap of her envelope.

So did the rest of the class.

They made loud, slurping noises.

Everyone laughed.

"Now, then, class, I'm going to lick the flap of another envelope," Mr. Merlin said.

Mr. Merlin turned his back to the class.

"Watch me carefully," he said.

He held up another envelope.

He licked the flap.

He turned back around to face the class.

"Which side of the flap did I start on?" he asked.

No one said anything.

It's a trick question, Noelle thought. She hadn't paid any attention to that.

She closed her eyes.

She tried to remember which side of the envelope flap Mr. Merlin had started on.

She then tried to remember which side of the envelope flap she had started on.

She thought she and Mr. Merlin had both started on the same side.

The left.

Noelle opened her eyes.

"The left?" she shouted.

"Correct!" Mr. Merlin said. "Now I'm going to give you another clue," he added. "I'm right-handed."

That's not much of a clue, Noelle thought.

Mr. Merlin looked at the class. "So what question would a good police detective ask next?" he said.

Chapter Six

Several people raised their hands.

Noelle couldn't believe it.

She didn't know the answer yet.

She held her breath.

"Put your hands down. I want everyone to think about it for a while. That's what a good police detective would do," Mr. Merlin said. "I'll ask you again after we've finished reading in our reader."

Noelle let out her breath.

She hoped Mr. Merlin didn't call on her to read.

She had to use that time to think up a question that a good police detective would ask next.

"Open your readers to page ten," Mr. Merlin said.

He looked around the class.

"Who wants to read first?" he asked.

Noelle ducked her head.

She pretended she was still trying to find page ten.

"I do," Amber Lee said.

Noelle looked up.

Oh, no! she thought.

Amber Lee must already know the next question a good police detective would ask.

Why would she waste her time reading if she didn't?

She'd be thinking about the question instead.

Of course, Noelle knew that Amber Lee liked to show off.

Amber Lee thought she was the best reader in the class.

Well, just let Amber Lee show off! Noelle decided.

When reading was over, Noelle would know the question, too!

Amber Lee started reading.

Noelle started thinking.

She thought about everything that Mr. Merlin had told them.

She thought about envelopes.

She thought about spit.

She thought about how Mr. Merlin had licked his flap from left to right.

She thought about how she had done the same thing.

She took a deep breath and then let it out.

Now what? she wondered.

She looked over at Todd.

Todd was following along in the reader as Amber Lee read.

Sometimes Noelle was so disappointed in Todd.

He should be thinking about the question, too.

Noelle sighed.

Had Todd licked his envelope flap from left to right? she wondered.

Suddenly, Noelle had an idea.

She poked Todd in the ribs.

Todd looked up.

"Show me how you licked your flap," Noelle whispered.

Todd rolled his eyes.

But he held up a *pretend* envelope.

He licked the flap.

Noelle felt her heart skip a beat.

"Do it again!" she whispered.

"No talking, please!" Mr. Merlin said.

Noelle turned.

Mr. Merlin was staring at her.

She pretended to cough.

Then she pretended to look at her reader.

After a few minutes, Amber Lee stopped reading.

Leon began reading.

Noelle was glad.

Mr. Merlin had to help him with every other word.

He would be too busy pronouncing words for Leon to notice what Noelle was doing.

Noelle gave Todd another poke.

"Lick your flap again," she whispered.

Todd rolled his eyes.

But he pretended to lick another envelope flap.

"That's it!" Noelle whispered. "I know what the question is!"

Chapter Seven

"Well, that's enough reading for today," Mr. Merlin finally said.

The class put away their readers.

Noelle looked over at Amber Lee.

Amber Lee still had a smile on her face.

Somehow, Noelle had to make sure Amber Lee wasn't the first one to tell Mr. Merlin what the question was.

She decided to take a chance.

"I know the question, Mr. Merlin," Noelle said. "Do you want me to tell the class?"

Amber Lee jerked her head around to look at Noelle.

Then she jumped out of her seat.

Her desk almost fell over.

"I know the question, too, Mr. Merlin," she

shouted. "It's 'Did a boy or a girl lick the flap of the envelope?'"

Noelle couldn't believe that Amber Lee had beaten her.

She looked over at Mr. Merlin.

Oh, please don't make that the question! she pleaded silently.

"Well, that's a good question, Amber Lee," Mr. Merlin said, "but I'm afraid that's not what a police detective would ask next."

He turned to Noelle.

"What do you think the question is?" he asked.

Noelle took a deep breath.

Here goes, she thought.

"I think the question is, 'Which side did the person start on when he licked the envelope flap?'"

"That's exactly right!" Mr. Merlin said.

Amber Lee started crying.

"What's wrong, Amber Lee?" Mr. Merlin asked.

"That's what I was going to say next," Amber Lee sobbed. "You didn't give me a chance to finish."

"Oh, I'm sorry," Mr. Merlin said. "Well, next time please remind me to give you more time to answer the question."

Amber Lee stopped crying.

"How can you find out which side the person started on?" Todd asked.

"You unseal the envelope flap scientifically," Mr. Merlin explained.

"Then you put special chemicals on it.

"I asked Dr. Smiley to test Amber Lee's envelope.

"The flap had more saliva on the right-hand side.

"It decreased across the arc to the left-hand side.

"That means whoever licked the envelope flap probably started on the right-hand side and licked to the left-hand side."

Mr. Merlin looked around the room.

"Think about it carefully," he said. "Which hand does this person probably use?"

Amber Lee raised her hand.

"He probably uses his left hand," she replied.

"Right-handed people usually lick envelope

flaps from left to right.

"Left-handed people usually lick envelope flaps from right to left."

"Excellent, Amber Lee!" Mr. Merlin said. He looked around the room. "I'm glad Amber Lee answered the question."

Noelle blinked. *Why?* she wondered.

"You'll all accomplish more if you work together," Mr. Merlin explained. "That's the way good police detectives do it."

Noelle bowed her head.

She knew Mr. Merlin was talking about her.

She raised her hand.

"Yes, Noelle?" Mr. Merlin said.

"I think we should all work together, too," Noelle said.

Amber Lee gave her a funny look.

But she didn't say anything.

Mr. Merlin smiled. "Well, I'm glad that's settled," he said. "Who knows what we have to do next in order to solve the mystery?"

Todd raised his hand.

"We have to find someone who's left-handed," he said.

"Excellent," Mr. Merlin said.

"That would help you narrow down who might have sent the letter.

"But it's important to remember that the envelope test isn't always accurate.

"Sometimes left-handed people start on the left.

"Sometimes right-handed people start on the right.

"Sometimes people start in the middle and lick to both sides.

"Most of the time, though, left-handed people start on the right, and right-handed people start on the left."

Mr. Merlin looked at the clock on the wall.

"Oh, my!" he said. "We need to do science and spelling before recess!"

So they spent the next hour learning about crocodiles and words that start with *sp*.

Then the bell for recess rang.

"We'll do math after recess," Mr. Merlin said. "Then we'll talk some more about our mystery."

Noelle stood up.

"I can't stand that Amber Lee!" she

whispered to Todd. "She made Mr. Merlin feel sorry for her. Now I think he wants her to solve the mystery!"

Todd grinned. "How can she solve the mystery if we solve it first?"

Chapter Eight

Noelle and Todd hurried outside.

All the other kids in their class were running around the playground, shouting, "Who's left-handed? Who's left-handed?"

"That's not the way to do it," Noelle said.

"Why not?" Todd said.

"Didn't you hear Mr. Merlin?" Noelle said.

"Not all people who are left-handed lick from the right.

"Not all people who are right-handed lick from the left.

"What we need to do is find people who lick from right to left no matter which hand they use!"

"Oh, yeah," Todd said.

Noelle looked over the playground.

She had forgotten that so many kids went to their school.

"We need some *suspects*," she finally said. She looked at Todd. "Do you think it's one of the other boys in our class?"

Todd shook his head.

"No. After Mr. Merlin told us how people licked envelope flaps, I saw Amber Lee ask the boys in the class to show her how they licked theirs.

"They licked them from left to right.

"And they're all right-handed, too.

"I went to sharpen my pencil while we were doing spelling so I could check everyone out.

"They were all using their right hands.

"But Leon needs to practice his cursive writing.

"I could hardly tell what the letters were."

"We have to think of *someone* who might have sent Amber Lee that letter," Noelle said.

"Well, she wasn't in our class last year," Todd said.

"She was in Mrs. Robertson's.

"Maybe it's one of the boys who was in her

class last year but who's in the other third-grade class this year."

"Yes, Todd! That has to be it!" Noelle cried. "I'm sure one of them wrote her that letter."

They ran to the middle of the playground.

They looked around.

Finally, Todd spotted the eight boys in the other third-grade class.

They were playing basketball.

"Let's test them," Noelle said.

She and Todd ran toward the basketball court.

"Hey, you guys. Stop!" Noelle shouted at them. "We have to talk to you!"

The boys stopped their game and stared.

"I'm going to give you a test," Noelle said when she and Todd reached the edge of the basketball court. "I want you to lick the flap of a pretend envelope."

The boys gave her a strange look.

But then they held up their pretend envelopes and licked the flaps.

Noelle watched them carefully.

They all started on the left-hand side.

That meant they hadn't licked the envelope that Amber Lee had received.

The bell rang to end recess.

The boys grumbled about not being able to finish their game.

Noelle and Todd headed back to their side of the building.

They stopped at the water fountain to get a drink.

The second bell rang.

"Oh, no!" Todd cried. "We're late for class!"

They ran down the hall.

They ran into the classroom.

The rest of the class had already started their math problems.

"You're late," Mr. Merlin said. He gave Noelle and Todd a stern look. "If this happens again, I'll have to send you to the office for a tardy slip."

Noelle felt so embarrassed.

She bowed her head.

She walked slowly down the aisle toward her seat.

She passed Leon's desk.

She stopped.

She couldn't believe what she saw.

Leon was doing his math problems with his *left* hand!

Chapter Nine

Noelle waited until they got to the cafeteria to tell Amber Lee what she had discovered.

"Leon sent you that letter," she said.

Amber Lee gasped. *"He did?"*

"Yes, he did," Todd said.

"How did you find out?" Amber Lee asked.

Noelle told Amber Lee what she had seen.

"I think he's really left-handed," she said. "I think he really licks envelope flaps from right to left, too."

"But I tested him!" Amber Lee said. "He licks envelopes from left to right."

"I think he *pretended* to lick envelope flaps from left to right," Todd said. "I think he *pretended* to be right-handed."

Amber Lee sighed. "Well, I can certainly

understand how someone like Leon would look up to me," she said.

Noelle looked around the cafeteria.

She saw Leon sitting at a table on the other side of the room.

But he wasn't eating.

He was staring at them.

Noelle, Todd, and Amber Lee stared back for several minutes.

Finally, Leon looked away.

He stood up.

He picked up his tray.

He put it on the conveyer belt.

Then he walked slowly by their table.

"You'll never prove it," he whispered.

Noelle and Todd looked at each other and grinned.

Amber Lee looked irritated.

During afternoon recess, Noelle and Todd cornered Leon on the playground.

They gave him their evidence.

Leon sighed.

"I thought I fooled you when I licked from

left to right," he said. "I normally lick from right to left."

"You fooled Amber Lee," Todd said.

Leon grinned.

"Did I also fool you when I wrote with my right hand?" he asked.

Todd nodded. "I just thought you couldn't write very well."

"Are you going to tell on me?" Leon said. "The other guys will all make fun of me if you do."

Noelle looked at Todd.

"What do you think we should do?" she asked.

Todd thought for a minute.

"We have to tell Mr. Merlin something," he finally said. "He has to know that we solved the mystery."

So Leon agreed to let them tell Mr. Merlin.

After school, the three of them stayed until everyone else was gone.

Mr. Merlin grinned when he heard what had happened.

"You let down your guard, Leon," he said.

"When you did your math, you weren't

thinking about which hand to write with, so you did what you *normally* do.

"You *normally* use your left hand.

"That's how a lot of criminals get caught.

"They let down their guard."

"You mean I'm a criminal?" Leon asked.

"No. No. Of course not," Mr. Merlin said. "I was just talking about *normal behavior.*"

Leon looked at Noelle and Todd.

"Don't forget," he said. "You promised you wouldn't tell anyone else."

Noelle and Todd looked at Mr. Merlin.

"The rest of the class will want to know the solution to the mystery, Leon," Mr. Merlin said. "We'll have to tell them something. Let me think about it overnight."

✉   ✉   ✉

The next morning, Mr. Merlin said, "Noelle and Todd have solved Amber Lee's mystery."

"Who sent her the letter?" Misty asked.

All of a sudden, Leon jumped up.

"I did!" he shouted.

The class gasped.

"I wasn't going to tell, because I was too

embarrassed," Leon continued. "But now I'm really excited about how the mystery was solved."

He walked to the front of the room.

"I talked to Mr. Merlin last night. He said our class can solve all kinds of mysteries like this. That's what I want to do."

"Us, too," several other kids said.

"Then that's what we'll do," Mr. Merlin said.

"There are lots of mysteries in our town that need to be solved.

"We'll solve them.

"We'll be the Third-Grade Detectives."

The class cheered.

"Of course, sometimes there are easier ways to solve mysteries like ours," Mr. Merlin said.

"We'll take a field trip tomorrow to the police laboratory to see how Dr. Smiley would have done it."

This was going to be the best third-grade class ever! Noelle thought.

She could hardly wait for tomorrow to come.

Chapter Ten

The next morning, Noelle and Todd got to school early.

A big yellow school bus was parked in front of the building.

Mr. Merlin said Amber Lee could get on first because it was her mystery that had started everything.

Amber Lee climbed up the steps.

She was wearing dark glasses.

When she reached the top step, she turned and waved to the rest of the class.

"Who does she think she is?" Noelle whispered to Todd. "A famous movie star?"

"Hurry up, Amber Lee!" Misty shouted.

Amber Lee gave her a dirty look.

The rest of the class climbed aboard.

Noelle and Todd sat down behind the bus driver.

The bus driver drove downtown.

He stopped the bus in front of a big building.

Noelle saw a sign.

It said, POLICE LABORATORY.

Mr. Merlin stood up. "Remember. We all need to stay together."

A man gave everyone a badge to wear.

The badges said, VISITOR.

Mr. Merlin led the class down a wide hallway.

He seemed to know all the policemen and policewomen in the building.

Finally, the class came to a really big room.

Dr. Smiley was waiting for them.

She was wearing a long white coat.

Noelle thought she looked like a doctor.

"Welcome to the Police Laboratory," Dr. Smiley said.

She pointed to all of the equipment in the room.

"These machines help me solve crimes.

"Mr. Merlin told me how Noelle and Todd solved the mystery of who sent Amber Lee the letter.

"He said it was someone in your class, but he didn't tell me who it was.

"I'm going to show you the way I'd solve the mystery.

"First, I'll start with the evidence.

"That's the flap of Amber Lee's envelope.

"Then I'll use one of these machines to analyze the saliva on it.

"It'll tell me about the DNA.

"Those letters stand for 'deoxyribonucleic acid.'

"It's sort of like building blocks for your body.

"Only one person in the whole world will have the same DNA as what the machine tells me."

"Next, I'll collect saliva samples from each of the suspects.

"That means everyone in the class."

Dr. Smiley gave each person a cotton swab to spit on.

She put each cotton swab inside a glass tube.

She wrote each person's name on the outside of his or her glass tube.

"You misspelled my name," Noelle whispered to Dr. Smiley.

"I'm sorry," Dr. Smiley whispered back.

She scratched out what she had written.

She wrote out "Noelle" correctly.

"Now, I'll use the machine to analyze each saliva sample," Dr. Smiley said.

"In two weeks, I'll tell you who sent the letter to Amber Lee."

Two weeks! Noelle thought.

She was disappointed.

She had hoped they'd find out right away.

Of course, she already knew.

And it hadn't taken her and Todd two weeks to find out, either.

Dr. Smiley took them on a tour of the rest of the laboratory.

She told them about fingerprints.

She told them about hairs and fibers.

She told them about blood.

She told them about fires and burns.

She told them about poisons.

She told them about guns and bullets.

She told them all about how police use science to solve crimes.

Noelle was very impressed.

She made sure she remembered everything.

⊠   ⊠   ⊠

Two weeks later, Dr. Smiley came to their classroom.

"We have a match!" she said.

She held up a cotton swab.

"The DNA of this saliva matches the DNA of the saliva on Amber Lee's envelope flap."

She looked down at the name on the glass tube.

"Leon Dennis!" she said.

The class applauded.

Noelle looked at Leon.

He looked embarrassed.

She remembered how he had tried to fool them by licking the envelope from left to right.

She remembered how he had tried to fool them by writing with his right hand.

He couldn't fool the DNA test, though.

"I have some good news, class," Mr. Merlin said. "Dr. Smiley enjoyed helping us solve Amber Lee's mystery. She'd like us to help her out the next time she has a mystery to solve."

The class let out a cheer.

Can You Break the Code?

Here's a secret message using the stacking code Mr. Merlin explains to the Third-Grade Detectives in chapter two of the book you've just read. But the stacks are in the wrong order! Can you rearrange the stacks and read the message?

P S A

Y X M

A I A

Oh, no! Here's ANOTHER message with the stacks in the wrong order. Can you figure this one out?

O N I G H

N E V E S

C T X E A

L O M E T

C K A B C

O E M T R

ANSWERS

The correct order for the first coded message is:

```
A I A
Y X M
P S A
```

Starting with X as the center of the clock, "I" is at noon, so the message is "I AM A SPY" (The "A" on the first line completes the square).

The correct order for the first coded message is:

```
C K A B C
O N I G H
L O M E T
C T X E A
O E M T T
N E V E S
```

Again, starting with X as the center of the clock, the "M" above X is at noon. Moving in a clockwise spiral, the message is "MEET ME TONIGHT AT SEVEN O' CLOCK" (the ABC on the first line completes the square).

Now that you're an expert decoder, have fun making up your own secret messages.